D0411150

nothing like a

For Keith and William

S. S.

For Olivia –

there's nothing like a daughter

B. K.

First published 2012 by Walker Books Ltd
87 Vauxhall Walk, London SE11 5HJ

10 9 8 7 6 5 4 3 2 1

This book has been typeset in Caecilia Heavy

Printed in China

British Library Cataloguing-in-Publication Data: a catalogue record for this book is available from the British Library

ISBN 978-1-4063-3581-1

www.walker.co.uk

puffin

SUE SOLTIS

illustrated by **BOB KOLAR**

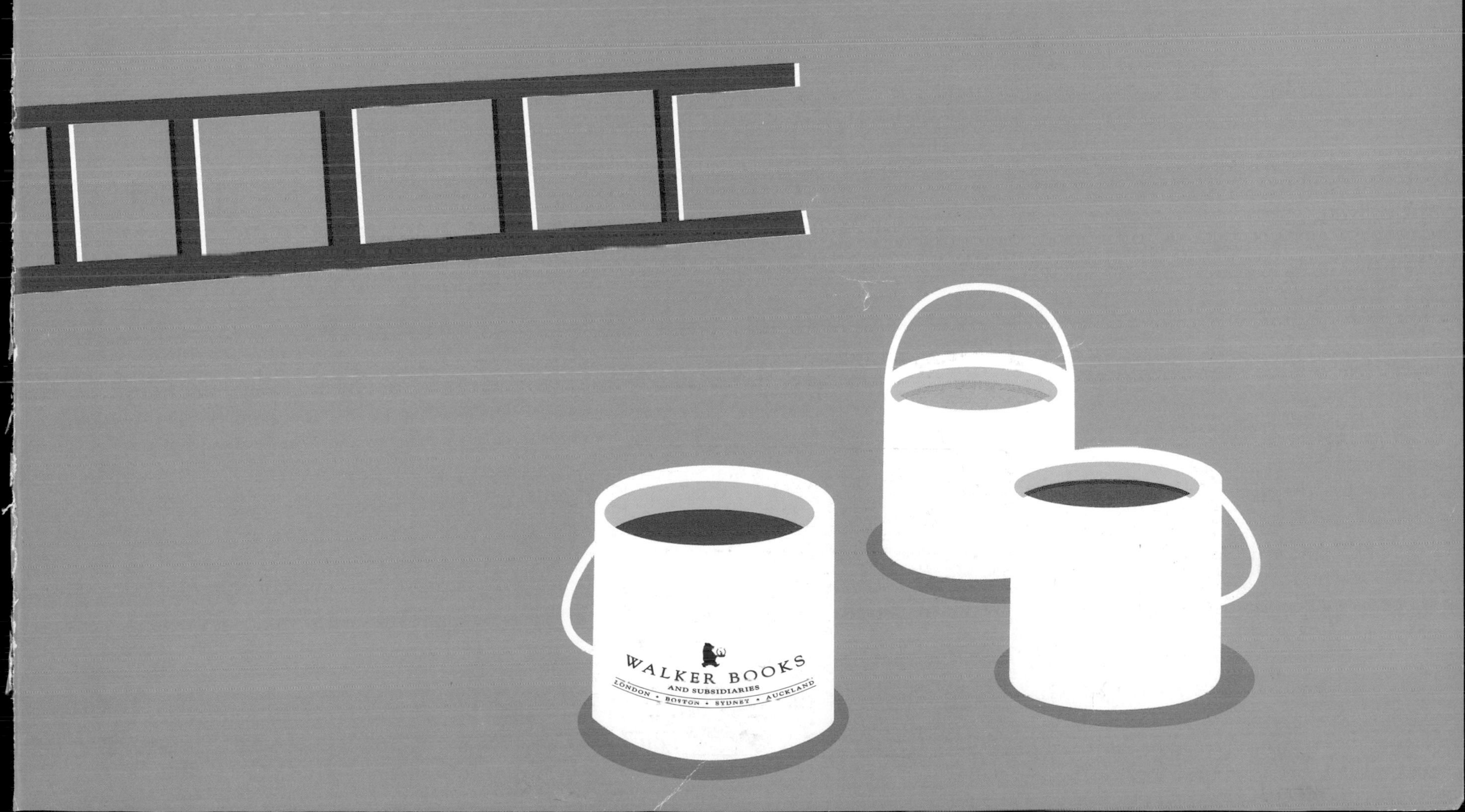

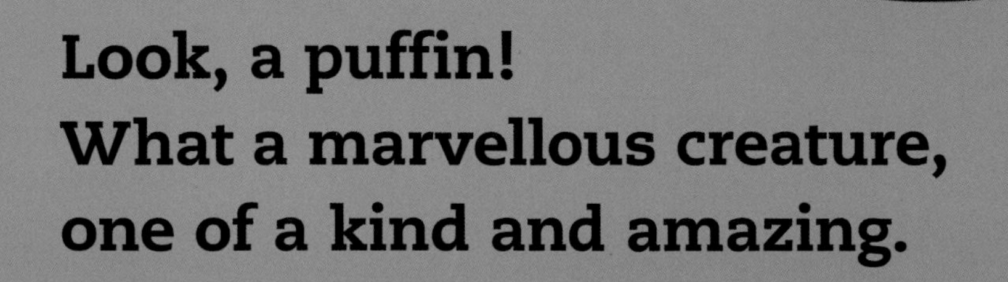

Look, a puffin!
What a marvellous creature,
one of a kind and amazing.

Indeed, there is nothing like a puffin.

Take, for example, this ladder.
A ladder is nothing like a puffin.
It has steps you climb up
to get somewhere high.

A house is also nothing like a puffin.
A house has windows and doors.

Inside are basins and chairs and beds.
A house is a place you can live in.

**A newspaper, to be sure, is nothing like a puffin.
A newspaper is shaped like a rectangle
and made out of paper.**

A newspaper has pages. It's black and white.

But wait –

a puffin is black and white, too!
Who would have thought it?

A newspaper is something
like a puffin, after all.

A pair of jeans, of course, is nothing like a puffin.
Jeans are blue.
Jeans have pockets and two legs.

Oh, no – don't say it.

Puffins have two legs, too!
Not another thing that's something
like a puffin...

Look out for the goldfish!

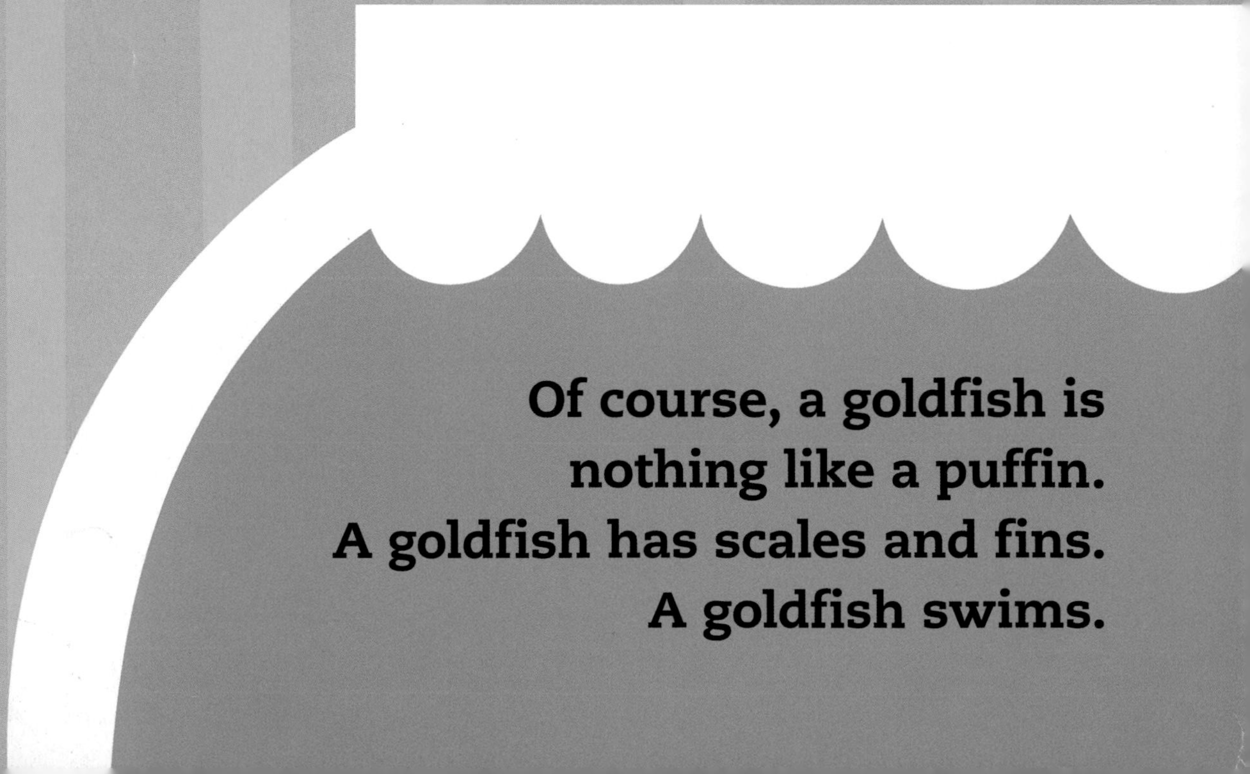

Of course, a goldfish is
nothing like a puffin.
A goldfish has scales and fins.
A goldfish swims.

It looks as if a puffin can swim, too.
A goldfish is a little bit,
a tiny little bit,
like a puffin.

So is a newspaper. So is a pair of jeans.
What could possibly be next?

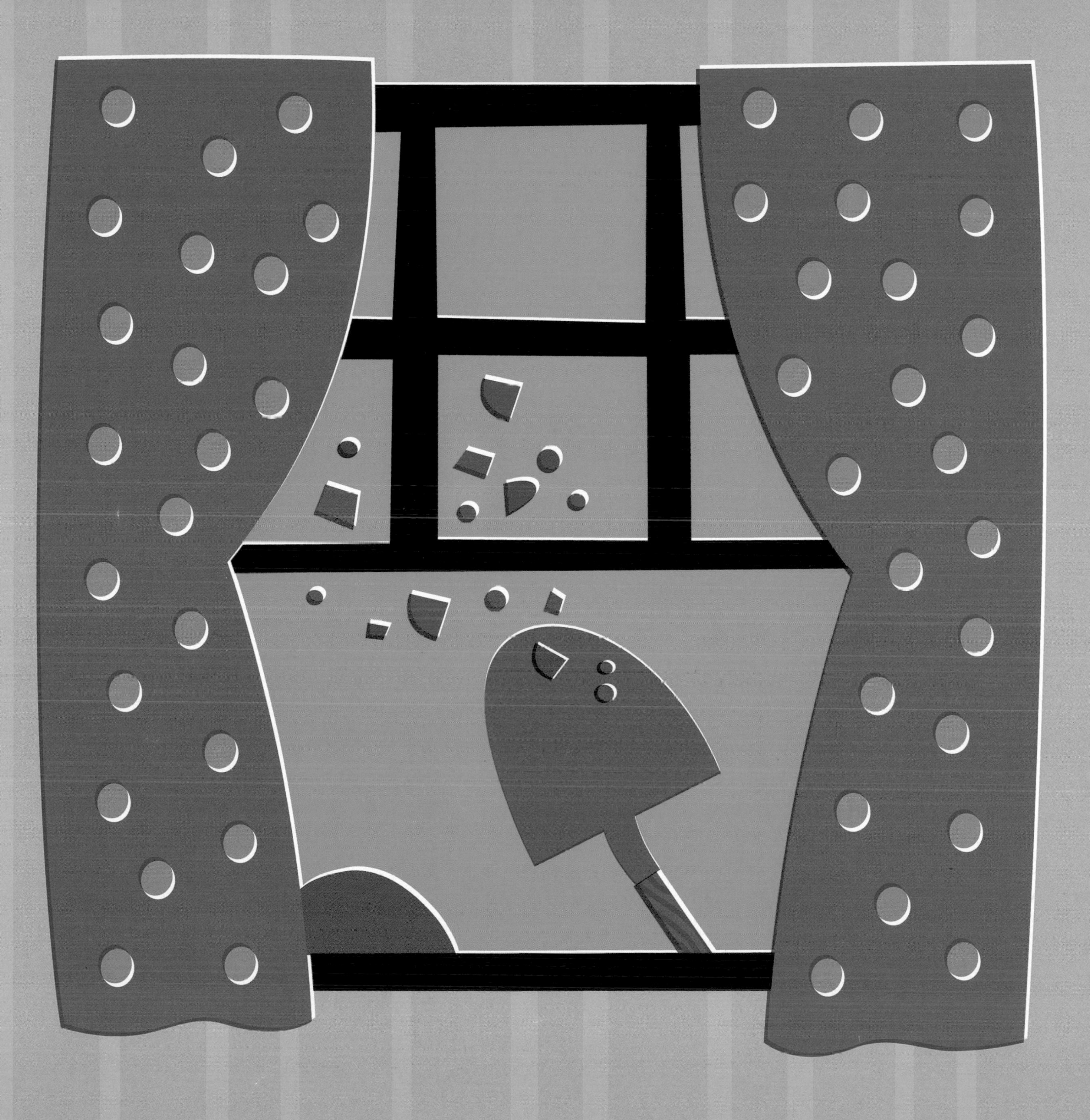

Surely a spade is nothing like a puffin.
A puffin isn't made out of wood and metal.
A puffin doesn't have a handle or a blade for digging.

Just a minute – a puffin uses its feet for digging.
A spade is a little something like a puffin.
Who would have guessed?

Look here, a snake is nothing at all like a puffin.
A snake moves along without legs or wings.
Snakes hatch from eggs, just like birds.

Wait a second...

A puffin is a bird!
So it must have hatched from an egg, too.
A snake is something like a puffin.

Oh, well.

What about that helicopter?

A helicopter doesn't have two legs.
And it can't swim.
It's made out of metal and has a propeller.
A helicopter flies.

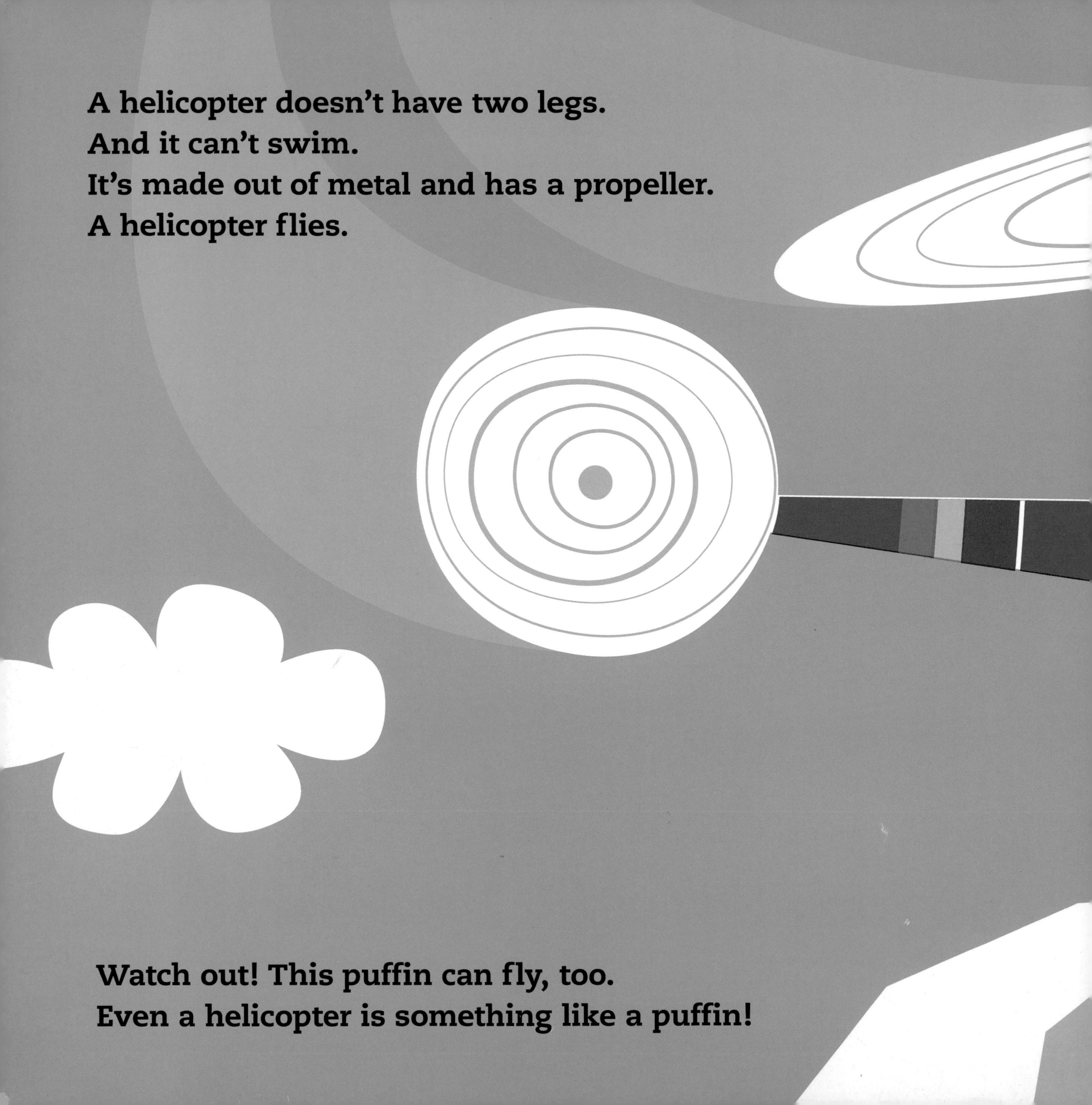

Watch out! This puffin can fly, too.
Even a helicopter is something like a puffin!

Maybe a puffin is not so amazing after all.
Maybe a puffin is not one of a kind.
Look at this penguin.

A penguin is black and white,
just like a puffin.
A penguin dives and swims.
So does a puffin.
A penguin is a bird.
So is a puffin.
A penguin has feathers
and two wings
and a beak
and two feet!

**There's no getting round it –
a penguin and a puffin are two of a kind.**

But look – a penguin can't fly!

A penguin is more than a little like a puffin – more than, say, a newspaper or a goldfish. But it's not *exactly* like a puffin.

So it's true!
It's true, after all!

There's nothing like a puffin!